Maggie's Treasure

Jon-Erik Lappano
Pictures by
Kellen Hatanaka

GROUNDWOOD BOOKS
HOUSE OF ANANSI PRESS
TORONTO   BERKELEY

Maggie had an eye for finding treasure.
Through parks, along pathways and in the
nooks of her neighborhood, she went hunting.
A dropped button, a bottle cap, a bright red
feather, a shiny stone ...

Maggie saw the sparkle in everything.

Her collection started small, as many things do. A tiny piece here, another bit there.

She filled a box.

Then a drawer.

Then a chest.

People in the neighborhood noticed the curious girl. They thought she was picking up trash. Ms. Pimms from next door praised her for it.

The city workers welcomed the help.
Hearing of Maggie's good deeds, even the
mayor presented her with a special award.

Over time, Maggie's appetite for treasure grew bigger.

And bigger ...

And bigger ... until Maggie's
collection had grown to an unreasonable size.

Treasure filled the cupboards,
corners and closets of her house.
It spilled out from under her bed.

Treasure hung from the trees and lay scattered across the garden. Her home stood out on the street like a menagerie of the strange and forgotten.

People in the neighborhood were beginning to talk.

Ms. Pimms no longer approved. With nothing left to clean up, the city workers were so bored they began grooming the squirrels. Complaints flew in to the mayor's office. Haunted by regret, the mayor was having trouble sleeping at night.

One afternoon, Maggie's parents spoke up.

"ENOUGH TREASURE!" her father said.

"THERE'S NO MORE ROOM!" said her mother.

Maggie stomped to her bedroom where she
sat and stewed like an emperor surrounded
by great piles of riches.

But looking around, even Maggie could see
that something had to be done.

What do people do with treasure? she wondered.

They hide it in caves and guard it with dragons. They sink it to the bottom of the ocean in treasure chests. They bury it and mark it with a giant X.

Considering her options, Maggie watched a bird pluck a shiny red ribbon from the bushes and carry it off to build its nest.

In that moment, Maggie knew what to do.

For days, a symphony of sounds
rang out from Maggie's garden.
The neighborhood buzzed with
curiosity. Ms. Pimms peered between
her rosebushes but couldn't get a decent
look. The city workers pruned some
nearby trees but the squirrels drove them
away. The mayor sent his assistant around to
investigate, but he went to the wrong house
and spent most of the afternoon hiding in a
garbage bin.

When Maggie finally stopped working, a
mysterious quiet hung in the air.
Posters appeared around the neighborhood.

MAGGIE'S TREASURE CHEST, they read.
FREE RICHES TO THOSE WHO SEEK THEM.

Slowly, cautiously, people began to arrive.
They stood in awe of Maggie's creation.

She'd crafted magic wands, painted stones, necklaces and rings. She'd made garden planters, bird feeders, mobiles and wind chimes. There were telescopes, kaleidoscopes, binoculars and monocles, music makers, rhythm shakers, kazoos, horns and drums.

Maggie's collection had been transformed, and it sparkled brighter than ever.
She invited her neighbors to help themselves to whatever they wished.

Ms. Pimms decorated herself from head to toe with jewelry fit for royalty. The city workers adorned the parks with bird feeders and wind chimes. Moved by the rhythm of tin-can maracas, the mayor danced his assistant through the streets.

The treasure spread throughout the neighborhood, each item finding a new home.

From then on, Maggie still spotted treasure wherever she went. Sometimes, she'd take an extra-special piece of it home and tuck it safely away in a small wooden box under her bed.

But most of the time, she'd smile and let it be, knowing it wouldn't remain there for long.

For Maia, Amelia and Ella,
who continue to fill our
home and our hearts
with treasure.
— JEL

For Tomo.
— KH

Text copyright © 2020 by Jon-Erik Lappano
Illustrations copyright © 2020 by Kellen Hatanaka
Published in Canada and the USA in 2020 by Groundwood Books

Groundwood Books / House of Anansi Press
groundwoodbooks.com

We gratefully acknowledge for their financial support of our publishing
program the Canada Council for the Arts, the Ontario Arts Council and
the Government of Canada.

 Canada Council   Conseil des Arts
for the Arts   du Canada

 ONTARIO ARTS COUNCIL
CONSEIL DES ARTS DE L'ONTARIO
an Ontario government agency
un organisme du gouvernement de l'Ontario

With the participation of the Government of Canada | Canadä
Avec la participation du gouvernement du Canada

Library and Archives Canada Cataloguing in Publication
Title: Maggie's treasure / Jon-Erik Lappano ; pictures by Kellen Hatanaka.
Names: Lappano, Jon-Erik, author. | Hatanaka, Kellen, illustrator.
Identifiers: Canadiana (print) 2019022813X | Canadiana (ebook) 20190228148 |
ISBN 9781773062372 (hardcover) | ISBN 9781773062389 (EPUB) |
ISBN 9781773064246 (Kindle)
Classification: LCC PS8623.A73745 M34 2020 | DDC jC813/.6—dc23

The illustrations were created digitally.
Design by Michael Solomon
Printed and bound in China

 FSC
www.fsc.org
MIX
Paper from
responsible sources
FSC® C144853